BizarreR Blunts

Written By:

Jamie Nichole

Time to get even more real. Thus, continue reading the poetic works of Jamie Nichole one, two, three, or several hits at a time. Each poem has different smoke forms to be inhaled according to your reading satisfaction. May you gain a piece of encouragement, laughter, or contagious puzzlement that inspires you to keep believing life is worth living despite trials and tribulations.

Freak in The Sheets

Just look at how he sleeps
He's smack dab in the middle of a twin bed
Can you see his covers wedged up his butt?
His legs are restlessly kicking the air
He is so ashamed, he sleeps face down
His headboard lost its cereal crown
Some nights, he sucks his grown-up thumb
Other nights, he dreams his dick were bigger
He has no clothes on for selfish reasons
So, don't bother trying to take off
what he doesn't have on

Gold Chainz

Invest in that which ye do not lust for
Own your own mental real estate
Sell what others think of your decisions
Keep buying space under the sun
Trade how you feel for the right thing to do
Count your lucky stars
Die to self

Sally Sue

How strange are you?
How much do you really weigh?
Why do your boobs want to come out and play?
Did you forget he slept with your sister?
Did you seal the deal with a gallon of ice cream?

Empire of Ducks

Your friends smell like the driest, dirtiest river,
like fart bombs that never expire
They roast you in public and private
and then lowly fly to a new pond

You're merely swimming on your own
You were wrong to trust their feathers
You were a total fool to follow their foul quacks
What you call friends are truly ugly ducks

Good mallards stay close to the edge
Good mallards don't let you drive drunk
Good mallards help you talk shit
Good mallards dazzle in the sun with you

Bad mallards splash you in your face
Bad mallards hold your beak under extra long
Bad mallards loiter the murky middle where snakes
nibble webbed feet
Bad mallards look out for their own fish

All empires contain a mix
All empires thrive on the mix
All empires sink when the mix is off
All empires have windows of choice

Pick the one that would never hang you out to dry
Pick the one that takes your bad with the good
Pick the one that pushes you the right direction
Pick the one that believes there is no ugly duckling

Courtyard My Front Yard

Gnome my bush with a colored glass globe on a stick
that leans like a bent dick
that has seen some ivy walls
all the way, half way, and none of the way covered
Navigate your way across broken stones
to the slew of artificial rainbow flowers
lining the window beds
that would otherwise be void of life
because the owner refuses
to water the sick seeds they plant

When they curse the lame patriotic neighbor,
who advertises on short sticks all they think matters,
keep traipsing passed the fake flowers
to encounter hedges hiding the disastrous foundation
where the dog urinates on the ant feuds
Don't go in the back yard
The front yard is where it's at
for those most concerned with curb appeal

Tater Tots

Shoot half shots
Wear burp cloths
Eat cups of applesauce
Wear pants filled with socks
Break obese limited shocks
that include ketchup dot to dots

Rings

Wear them on any finger
Flip people off with the usual finger
Act like you're faithful on the ring finger
Celebrate the gooch
with a piercing that takes the cake

Where are You?

I'm hearing so many sounds
while trying not to make a sound
My tummy is getting hungry
I might start acting funny
I'm thinking about eating fingers,
but that might get me in trouble

Trouble bad
Hungry bad
So bad
Too bad
No

My Tires Expired

The tread is completely gone
The rubber is burned
Might start a road fire
Yet, I still keep driving
Somehow, the wheels miraculously stay on

What-a-melon

Turns tons of heads
Should never wear dreads
Just look at those legs
Should take her to bed
Best juice in the house
Too big for her house
She sat in the tree instead
to look down on all the weenies

Miss Piggy

She believes in baby Jesus
She doesn't take no for many answers
She smells as divine as southern ham
She never cooks with Pam
She never sleeps with Mr. Clean
Her dreams are boring
Her favorite food is bread
Her last boyfriend was the biggest loser
Her standards last for seconds
Her name has nothing to do with her ass

Beer in Winter

Frosty mugs of don't cook dinner
Tons of wins and losses
Too many dudes in a garage
Make an old man's beard quiver
Friends soaking up brown splendor
Wondering what's for dinner
Best if opened by mid-November

Do You Love Me?

Without makeup?
In spite of enlarging marks?
Even if I accidentally fart?
When I can't keep myself in check?
If my blood makes a mess?
Whether or not I shave my legs?
When I clean both our plates?
As much as God loves me?
From as soon as you met me?
Always, no matter what?
Please say yes!

Precisely

In the middle of the couch
In the middle of the bed
In the middle of the movie
In the middle of an argument

On show me lane
On season two of nobody knows
On the trip of a lifetime
On fire in my brother's kitchen

Beside a big pimple
Beside the cat's bowl
Beside my middle finger
Beside the biggest cupcake ever

Nobody cares.

Find Me A Senorita

I need a second mommy
that makes me blow my nose
and wipes my ass before and after dinner

Who cuts my food into manageable pieces
Who shakes my dick with the right grip
Who swallows all the bad I come at her with

You know the one
The one who eats loveless bean burritos
and drinks lifeless piña coladas
Nice and ready to become a momma-rita

Take Me Now

This is how it must go down
I get one and you get two
Drive the stick to where we
both wipeout naked
ending up with one more kid
who keeps us home for dinner
while all the joy grows inside
keeping the love spicy hot

Doing You

Hair that never cares
Underwear stealing stares
Lips that say whatever you want
Drive faster than you should
Eat your fantasy menu
Sleep with no eyes open
Take your own self out
Turn the a/c on
Turn the a/c off
Cuss in the wind
Be your best friend
Die eating cake

Oprah Winfree

You get a job
You get some money
You get a car
You go to Disneyland
You all go to heaven

Hardcopy

A hard copy is a hardcopy
It's not a soft copy
because it's a hardcopy
I knew better than to give you a hardcopy
My files are now corrupt
because I didn't give you up
My screen is all jacked up
The delete key is conveniently stuck
I told you it's a hardcopy
You pressed enter anyway
Once you've shared,
there's no room for backspacing
That's the way you suck the life out of a soft copy
who will never be a hardcopy

Sharpie

They smell kinda nice
They write fairly well
They love to change color
They will leave a stain
They make sure you know names
They are never going to change
They will just keep leaving their mark

People on their Phone

Fake nice
Wave their hands
Forget they're driving
Roll their eyes
Studder
Cuss
Cry
Sympathize
Realize
Pick their nose
Say hell no
Take a dump
Take a pee
Give their kid a thump
Make new friends
Say I'm sorry
Propose to Charlie
Tune the world out
Force a fart
Talk too loud
Think they're cool
Feel important

Nail Done

Karen is at the nail salon
She got seated right beside you
She will ruin more than your experience
You can try to tune her out,
but she has a really big and unruly mouth

Karen barks at the nail techs
even though her toe nails are so bad,
they require acrylics
She manages to be overtly rude while
simultaneously catching up on
her never forsaken social media

Karen thinks everyone else sucks
Everyone knows she's a bitch on purpose
All the nail salon employees catch on to her bullshit
antics and start to talk mad shit about
her in mandarin and Vietnamese

Karen is a disease you can't treat
Just do your best to keep three feet distance
Throwing her a bone is not worth it
She is only here to devour
what you thought would be a golden hour

Hair Done

Hair color smells like ass,
but we be doing it errry four to eight weeks
anyway
We know it won't last
We know it's fake pigment
We ain't foolin nobody
anyway
Takes tons of time
Some like sitting on their ass waiting
for their hair color to set
Some grow more gray hairs while waiting
anyway
Color, color, color, color me
Hello beautiful
anyway
Truth is, you and your hair are wasting away
Go ahead and keep fighting a losing battle
anyway
Gray wins

Don't Fuck with Me

I'll mess you up
if you don't shut up
I don't play with small town
homies like you bruh

Tired of your bogus lies
and afro decorated with sneezes
ain't no room for saying sorry
you might just wanna go ahead and run

Head home to your big ass momma
I don't play in these streets
even though it's where I learned
my trifling abc's

You took my hoe
So, we are passed taking it outside
She wore that thong for me
So, let's see whose sword can really make her scream

Goodbye Tom

How's your mom?
Did she lose her mind?
I need you to know
I don't care who you blow
Fuck me street is dark
Fuck me street is zoned for double cops

Arrest your blessed up soul
God only knows your every move
You should let him inside you
Otherwise, you might die and rise to suffer alone
There are always two options
You took the one that requires a faulty front

We wished we had a bigger ass
to twerk you outta being a fucking jerk
How's grace supposed to wash you?
You refuse to get clean
It's my turn now to own this street
Goodbye Tom

Saw My Teacher

Seeing Ms. was real
She always smells like applesauce
Ms. shook my parent's hands
I stared to the side to hide
Her face is always tired
Why does she do what she does?
If I were her, I'd be so over that gig
I finally realized, she was born with a first name
I'll call her boss, despite her professional loss
at making more than necessary money

Seeing her shop, was freaking funny
Who knew she eats food too?
I thought she only consumed chocolate
Ms. has her own kids too
I definitely thought we were it
Now, my video watching mind needs to split
My teacher still needs to grade my test
Watch me flex my attitude,
while she consistently gives her best
Yo, I'm about to post this

Gamer's Roar

Nooooo!
Why'd you do that bruh?
I'm about to throw my remote
This is the last time I ask you to play

Nooooo!
You just killed my guy
I'm not giving you the secret code now
Dude, take your Mario Bros home

Trippin on Rosemary

Found a hair in my Chick-Fil-A
Yep, I ate it anyway
Then, I slurped on a Sonic slushie
found on the side of a dirty water fountain
Next time, I hope to find a room temp piece of pizza

Time to go home to Lisa
I'd rather eat days old meatloaf
At least I know how to lay her
down to sleep at night
where we keep each other warm

She has the bigger appetite
Tomorrow, I'll go back out
to the strip
where I met
plus size Mona Lisa

Penis Feather

Across the face
Beneath the chin
Balls start the count down from ten
Down the chest
Across the belly
I'm a lucky jelly
Once past the pelvis,
take off the teddy
Now, fly away lil birdie

Balls are Annoying

They get cold
They get horny
They are prickly
They shrivel up
They get kicked
They eat sweat
They hang uneven
They need scratching
They hold babies
They make weird bulges
They must be lifted when washing
They get old fast
They smell rancidly dumb
Don't you want to own a pair?

Who's in Charge?

I'm getting new tits today
I'll be better able to slay into my desired way
Tits and bums rule the world
Some only follow tits
Some only follow bums
Both take you to the same place
One might get you there faster
I'm so excited to point my rockets
The sky will be the limit with these babies

Feelin Funny

I'm scared
I'm not right
I'm not swell
I'm thinking of all I've done wrong
Maybe I'm going manic,
but I don't want to
Help me calm down inside
by showing me all your knives
I don't care who knows
I don't have that kind of pride
I am going ninety miles per hour inside
Take this fucking seat belt off me
I'm ready to crash with you by my side
I feel better with you
Is that how you feel too?

Greetings

Hey!
Hi!
Ho!
Hola!
Bonjour!
How are you?
Fuck you!
What's up?
Say there…
What's new?
What's good?
Who are you?
Yo!
Oh, hell no!
Sup?
Nice to meet you!
Go to hell!

Violin Me

Don't forget to send me on a musical trip
to pita chips and strings of hummus
I like crawling under your chin,
that's how I see under your nose
Some chords make my mind quiver
How come you play with a surprised look on your gut?
It makes me obey King Tut
He demands I play Chaconne in D minor
When I was holding out for Concerto in D major
to strike lightening into your loins
Take a bow and then return to your seat in the back
where you can't properly see the conductor of your
questionable sex life

True Dat

Man-buns are out
Skinny pants remain
Reality tv isn't real
Women wear metaphorical pants
Albert Einstein's hair is weird
People smell of invisible dust
Guns will always be dangerous
The government is more and more corrupt
Cheese on boards for the win
Tacos make an appearance on
more than just stupid Tuesdays
Cake makes you fat, but temporarily happy
Naked animals poop outdoors
Old people fall in the bathtub
Joey eats pizza everyday
Roses cause sore thumbs
Teenagers feel cool in their first car
Warm beer is gross
The truth often hurts

All Night

We'll sit and watch people
openly white stare
at black matters
that actually have our backs

Everything is not an atomic attack
Some ants just need to build
what other abnormalities
can't wake up and ignore

Pull My Finger

Would you like to smell what I had for dinner?
Or would you like to smell the
aftermath of what I had for dinner?

Would you like to see me dance like a drunk beaver?
Or would you like to keep acting
like you're beaver cleaver?

Would you like to hear me sing cry me a river?
Or would you like to skip rocks
on top of a lazy river?

Would you like to hear me say it or spray it?
Or would you like to find
ten pieces of gum on your toilet seat?

Would you like to win a million blue psychedelic stuffed
teddy bears?
Or would you like me to
confess my sins committed just this morning?

Road Trip

Fuel the bod and not the car
Clean the seats and not the sheets
Change the oil, but not the sexual performance
Check the air then say a prayer
Pack the snacks and leave the cat
Charge the phone and not your dick
Take first-aid because you drink adult Gatorade
Fasten your seat belt since mom's driving
Shave your feelings, but make sure you're speeding
Leave behind familial gas,
so your tank has room for new memories

Nothing's Wrong

I'm just weird
I'm just loud
I'm just proud
I'm just fine
I'm just shy
I'm just super clean
I'm just picky
I'm just ambidextrous
I'm just a freak in the sheets
I'm just the life of the party
I'm just a good cook
I'm just beyond beef
I'm just a good gossip starter
I'm just right and you're wrong
I'm just a fan of pink
I'm just me
We love you

Barbie-Cue

Snap out of it, mister
She's not into you
You think you're the one
She flirts with everyone
She has no intent
beyond what you see
She's plastic all the way through
She doesn't bite upfront
She is late to reveal,
how she actually feels
Go find some authentic sauce instead

I'm Hurting

Thoughts of you kill me
Not because I don't love you
The reverse is true
I'm struggling with losing you
I held on as long as I could
Now my soul is black and blue,
all related to losing you
I can't sleep at night
I'm tormented by pleasant memories
I still see you
I still hear you
I still smell you
I still need you
Yet, I can't have you
You took me to the moon
Now, I'm lost looking for Mars
Mars is unreachable
Please come back soon,
I will die without you

No Sleep

I want to sleep
My body says no
I rise half dead after listening to the world sleep
I don't know how to make amends with the sleep lost
Very few get it
It's all the worse when you don't know how
to go about the day a smiley dead clown
with an internal frown that's a
blister of the wee hours taunting
Please don't stare at my hair
Give me mercy and grace
It may seem undue
Just try to think past you
Just try to realize how lying awake at night,
is a surreal punishment often undeserved

Walk of Shame

Why are you ashamed?
You chose to do it
You so totally enjoyed it
You so want to tell everyone about it
Can't wait till next time

How I regret it now
Why'd I do it?
I can't undo it
They're talking about me
Wish I wouldn't have done it

Got to make peace with it
Can't let it eat me alive
Don't want to cry anymore
Time to let it go and ask myself
What can I learn from it?

Them

They have strong opinions
They prevent you from doing what you really want
They decide the latest trend
They don't care if you agree with them
They lead you to doubt everything
They sell what works for them most
They refuse to listen to reviews
They show up unannounced
They squash your mind of your own
They leave the last drop of nothing
They wait until you're not ready
They cook for themselves
They forget there's a rug by the door
They prefer you at your absolute worst
They will likely steal your purse
They trade nothing for something
They are all around

Fried Cake

Doesn't work
Doesn't wait
Doesn't skate
Doesn't fluff
Doesn't thick
Doesn't sit right
Doesn't sound right
Doesn't taste good
Doesn't digest
Doesn't make sense
Doesn't say happy birthday
Doesn't create the right sensation
Doesn't make babies
Doesn't belong on the menu

Windmills

Have three sleek legs
and a concealed bidet in the middle
All parts are standing on a pixie stick
The rotation occurs slowly
as if churning air into energy butter
They stand in groups or far apart
posing as modern bleak flowers with no soul
because they are devoid of personality
Each shares the same name and purpose
The saddest part is that only the sun can ride them

You Suck

All you do is fuck shit up
Why did you even show up?
My mom told me not to come,
but I thought it best not to suck my thumb
You fucking blew it once again
Don't say my name that way again
I'll have you know I'm not your friend anymore
You took your top off and screwed my current crush
Shame on you for being so zeal
Your character is non existent
I totally thought you were worth much more
It turns out, your nothing but a typical whore

Bad Service

You wait ten years for what's free
They delay bringing you what you really craved
How busy they were on the day of the month
your vagina let out all its creamy junk
Red is such a dread when she brings undeniable pain
No one has patience
for people living their life to hurt others
Take your lack of basic human decency
and shove it up your privileged butt
Who cares if you care?
It's all a big scam
Show your ass and I'll show you mine
That will be the end of you

Grow a Dick

It's time for your balls to drop
No more messing around
Big things grow
when you learn to let go
Leave your safety den
Rise seven inches north
of where you last shot hoops
Fear is here, there, and everywhere
Feel yourself catapulting vertically
Tell your inhibitions to take the bench
Almighty knows your size, eyes, and heart
He never has to smell your farts
He loves you no matter what,
even on the days you fail to shave
Lay your shadow at the right set of feet
Check your fly to protect the seed
You're about to explode atop Mount Rushmore

Home Wreckin

Do you like it when I fart naked?
Do you like it when I pick my nose in the car?
How about when my crack is out?
Got to jet, takin her to see an imposter Led Zepplin

Hair Around the Nipple

It's in the way of what you want
It grows back ten times thicker
It's not good to eat two dinners
It stares you down while you eat tuna
It's not invited to the next party
It builds a fortress around indecision
It's cyclical in nature
It won't take yes for an answer
It's whatever color it wants to be
It refuses to wash its hands before dinner
It's the worst place to call home

Mumus

The best dressed Shamu
The hairiest Shamu
The biggest mouthed Shamu
The shortest Shamu
The bad eye shadow Shamu
The spider vein Shamu
The Vaseline based Shamu
The pointy busted Shamu
The Summer's Eve Shamu
The over the hill Shamu
The wrinkled neck Shamu
The floral smelling Shamu
Hey, you know Grandma

Your Mom's Middle Finger

You never noticed how bitter she is,
until you turned twenty
At that point, you saw the bitterness buildup
How it spanned across all of your twenty years
Even though it's not your fault,
you tried your best to please her
All you ever saw was the dark circles of dread
All you heard was her pleas for her dead mother's milk
She's not all mad, so it's understandable
that she had you fooled into thinking she cared
Your concern is that she will die bitterest of all
Your prediction is she dies flipping off the one who
denied her love every night
The truth is, she will lay in the ground
crying dry tears from every bad name
they called her when she didn't slightly deserve it
If only she could have heard it
without feeling the lethal verbal cuts
such as calling her a no-good slut
Her heart for life stopped beating long before she had her
first child who turned out really wild
Grab her hand and force down her middle finger
Don't throw the dirt on her until it's not sticking up
This is the only way to save her children
from becoming suicidally bitter too
Bitter is the supreme middle finger
some never understand
So, to the ones who do,
Make sure you tell your mom you love her

Taking Sides

Such a hard thing to do
Especially when one side isn't you
Unfortunately, you must pick a side
Go with who told the truth
Oops, that wasn't you

Bra Cuffs

You really suck all the juice out of muscles needed
to avoid looking masculine
You never fit the right way
I sweat inside you
He tries to see through you
Meanwhile, you don't know how to do a proper push-up
All day, I can't wait to unsnap you
Breaking free requires double d's I'll never have
Lock me back up so I can go for my run

Bitches in Tahoes

Pull out in front you driving at least five kids around
who could half belong to someone else
down, down Yuppie Lane they go
just having finished a play date
hello, didn't see you there
My mom's butt is bigger than yours, so you'll need to
understand, I'm better than you
My man is taller than yours, so I unapologetically
pulled out in front of you
Aren't you glad to see my university status symbol while
you drive behind me?
My dad paid for my down payment on my house,
I feel uniquely entitled to let my kid hit your car door
Don't you know, that's what you get
for not being better than me
See you on the mediocre streets

Respectfully, Bitch in The Tahoe

Hello world
I drive a big SUV
I sit close to the steering wheel
Honestly, a man should be driving this rig
My fake chest almost touches the airbag
Good thing my belly is held in by Spanx
I actually made dinner last night
My kids didn't even cry while they ate it
Driving with my bright lights on
is my favorite way to see speedbumps
To me, your car is Willy Wonka
while mine sits high like a Tonka
I'm about to meet my sugar daddy
at the newest yuppy spot
So glad you can't afford to go there too
No Honda is allowed in my garage
I ride dirty while looking purdy
Can't wait to hit the curb driving passed
all the no name nerds
Honk if you agree that I'm sexier than you

Sleepovers

All screams and no dreams
Pleas for more screen time
Vanilla colored ice cream
Chips everywhere
Stares from mom
Dares from dad
No homework
No sleeping
Supersonic butt and mouth sounds
Twerps that will have uber chores tomorrow

Don't Date My Mom

She's the same age as your mother
She has two military brothers
She silently farts undercovers
She is no longer fertile
She once made out with a turtle
She will cause too many monetary hurdles
She's more than twice your age
I once sucked her boobs

Don't Date My Dad

He is an unbeliever
His bent is fruity flavored wine
He treats black people bad
He'll never open any door
He splits apart his Oreos
He smells like foreign laced cigars
His chihuahua cries in his lap
I will always be his favorite princess

Biceps, Triceps, Back

Check out my biceps
Followed by my triceps
back
To me, it's always about
me
I spent two hours at the
gym today
all so I could flex for you
back
Some years ago, I left my
spine behind
All I need are biceps
The right is bigger than the
left
My triceps are an added
bonus
back
Then I used to not care if
anyone stared
I developed a life size
Cheeto of an ego
I discovered all the fish in
the sea
back
To how everyone needs to
look at me holding the
smallest things

Accentuating my biceps is
a full-time job
My worm is not as big my
arm guns
back
To the future when my bis
and tris cook dinner for
you
Oh crap, I forgot to work
my joystick out as much as
my arms
So, now we only meet for
lunch
back
Home is where my mom
helped me grow into a big
asshole
sporting nothing but one
and a half biceps and some
triceps no one gives a
damn about
back
Up your car into every
parking spot like me
Keep your arm bent like
me
That's how people view
the show with never
ending douche bag
episodes
back

My Lil Psycho Pony

I feed her strips of bacon
to keep her rainbow bright
and strong to ride all night
through the streets of Paraguay
I caught her humping the neighbor's fern
I had to teach her all about beating the right bush
to avoid losing my best friend to a neighborly gun shot
She breaths locks of starburst gummies so juicy
she ends up burping musical notes
that make everyone want to float
above donkey's asses found driving on
the black and white highway
To hell she's headed for all the crazy rides she has given
For now, I keep her by my side even though
she is coo-coo for coco puffs
If you promise to spank Starry Bright's ass just right,
she'll be your best friend for life

Constipation

What keeps you up at night?
How long since you last went?
You sit on the pot all day,
but nothing ever comes out
You keep everything bad in
It would do you much good
to drop all the weight you're carrying
Take a load off so we can see the real you
that's hiding behind dung built up over time
as you collected wasteful memories
that clung to your tubes
Open your mouth and we'll insert
the hose that knows the right
number of apologies to send your bowels
running out the other end
Make sure you flush next time you release all you ate
while thinking other people
would help you flip the poop fan on

Addicted to Nic

Exposed early on
to what's supposedly freer than
traditional stinky cigs
Pods of glory supposedly meant to bring freedom
Trapping you in addiction
nearly impossible to break free from
It might not stink, but it will bring you nic sickness
You will want to projectile vomit
the mistakes you put in your mouth
thinking it was just what you needed to help
you chill amidst Covid ramifications
What a false loop of resurrection promise
Kids need love, not a hit of vaporization
that leaves them wanting more of what will never
help them fulfill their potential
Let's get real and help them say goodbye to their jewel

Wine

A cup will do you right
Two cups will do you even better
Three cups will get you talking stupid
Four cups will send you to the dance floor
Five cups will make you take your clothes off
A whole bottle will make the most incredible pee
Two bottles will make you wake up next to a bum

Cookie Sabotage

You know you're not allowed in here
I told you to stay away
I saw you in the store,
but I broke up with you days ago
Go find another mouth
There are so many other mouths in the sea
It's totally personal at this jar
I can't afford any more pounds
of dough sticking to my thighs
Now is when I cry because things could have worked out
If only you went straight to my chest,
but that's not how the cookie crumbles

Wiping My Butt

I went poop today
That means I fondled some trees afterward
It's a glorious feeling
when you wipe the dirty away
I don't fold my tree leaves up
I bunch my tree up as if I am powdering my nose
It usually takes a few trees to wipe clean
The reward is on the other side
of stinky business excretion
It's called-standing up, flushing,
and letting all that shit go
Your turn

Sex Here, There, Everywhere

Do you smell it in the air?
I see through all their underwear
What lies beneath never sleeps
There is too much external stimulation
creeping into my mind then pants
How do I avoid all the sextification?
We are all worthy of hell
Some don't care, while others do
Yet, all we see is sex here, there, everywhere

Dad Jokes

Completely lame
Laugh anyway
Drive you insane
Fart in your ears
Worth a fist bump
Belong on a shirt
Make good memes
Always passed around
Get old
Turn mom off
Embarrass the kids
Change the subject
Make the stuck up roll their eyes
Go great with fries
Piss the widowed neighbor off
Born out of truth
Deserve a salute
Make the dog bark
Best served in the car
Take too much time to tell
Leave you shaking your head
Call for lucid understanding
Don't deserve shunning
Grow hair on the youngest chest
Should close in prayer
Don't make you pee your pants
Are always up your sleeve
Never ending
Call for back up

Walking Invisible Dogs

The wrong relationship requires
leashes
The right relationship
unleashes
The wrong pair of shoes
leashes
The right pair of shoes
unleashes
The wrong direction
leashes
The right direction
unleashes
The wrong salad dressing
leashes
The right salad dressing
unleashes
The wrong amount of sugar
leashes
The right amount of sugar
unleashes
The wrong weather
leashes
The right weather
unleashes
The wrong sound
leashes
The right sound
unleashes
The wrong house
leashes

The right house
unleashes
The wrong color
leashes
The right color
unleashes
The wrong underwear
leashes
The right underwear
unleashes
The wrong smell
leashes
The right smell
unleashes
The wrong investment
leashes
The right investment
unleashes
The wrong attitude
leashes
The right attitude
unleashes

Drinking Invisible Tea

Swallowing the wrong information
dehydrates you
Swallowing the right information
fills you up
Swallowing lies
dehydrates you
Swallowing truth
fills you up
Swallowing false hope
dehydrates you
Swallowing unconditional love
fills you up
Swallowing bullshit marketing
dehydrates you
Swallowing unbiased promotions
fills you up
Swallowing unsolicited advice
dehydrates you
Swallowing experiential feedback
fills you up
Swallowing second hand facts
dehydrates you
Swallowing firsthand knowledge
fills you up
Swallowing what they think of you
dehydrates you
Swallowing your virtues
fills you up
Swallowing what you should have done
dehydrates you

Swallowing a second chance
fills you up
Swallowing bubble gum compliments
dehydrates you
Swallowing genuine thoughts
fills you up
Drink only what's real

4 Reel

My latest post was TMI
My latest post was LOL
My latest post was #weird
My latest post was FML
My latest post was DIY
My latest post was SMH
My latest post was LMAO
YOLO

Get Off the Road

Forgot the turn signal
Forgot to turn quicker
Forgot to stay in my own lane
Forgot to turn my lights on
Forgot to not pull out in front of people
Forgot to leave my wife at home
Forgot to avoid the curb
Forgot to stop at red lights
Forgot you had the right of way
Forgot to give the other cars space
Forgot to keep my eyes on the road
Forgot to do my make up at home
Forgot to at least go the speed limit
Forgot to check my mirrors
Forgot the cup had no lid
Forgot where I parked
Forgot you might not like my music
Forgot where the fuck I am going

I'll Drink to That

The cat didn't throw up
The roaches went
somewhere else
The package came on
time
The picture turned out
nice
The kite actually flew
The kitchen is all
cleaned up
The neighbor moved
The right shoe fits
The mayor is a uniballer
The light came on
The bitch didn't stay
The pants still fit
The in-laws live pretty
far away
The stench went away
The plane landed
The car has plenty of
gas
The donut isn't
chocolate

The cow is pregnant
The door wasn't locked
The bill is finally paid
The store's still open
The cheese tastes better
than it smells
The pimple isn't here
forever
The month isn't May
The girl took her top off
The sex is good
The day isn't done
The extra pounds came
off
The dream came to pass
The paycheck was more
than fat
The sin can be forgiven
The baby was finally
born
The fun is still to come
The poem is finally over

The Mall

Let's go to the mall
says no one in a thong
Let's go to the mall
says the boy who wants to flirt
Let's go to the mall
says the unapologetic shopaholic
Let's go to the mall
says the introvert
Let's go to the mall
says the mother of five under five
Let's go to the mall
says friendless Fred
Let's go to the mall
says the one who needs only one thing
Let's go to the mall
says the one looking for a free massage
Let's go to the mall
says the friend you dread
Let's go to the mall
says the one not paying
Let's go to the mall
says the one still in bed
Let's go to the mall
says the one with a gun
You still want to go?

Yes Ma'am

Say it or else
By the time I count to three
You'll see I'm mean
Respect is just given, not earned
I'll spank your ass so hard,
you'll wish I hadn't
reached three strikes
Never forget to say yes ma'am

Yes Sir

You can do that
You can say that
You can fart that
You can buy that
You can drive that
You can fry that
You can tap that
You can drink that
You can live there
You can go there
No sir, you can't have me

Fat Girlz

Smell like donuts
Snort when they laugh
Eat everything in sight
Elevate the insurance rate
Pick sizes too small
Pray to be skinny
Wait the longest wait to be seated
Wish healthy food erased the shame
Die happy

Time to Go

They never wanted you
You wanted them
They mix up your name
You put them first
They run your name through the dirt
You say, how high?
They don't even jump
You feel their feelings
They have none
You think they hung the moon
They think you're run of the mill
You bring them gifts
They bring you sadness and pain
You say sorry
They say it was because of you
You give them the last bite
They make sure you get none at all
You know what makes them smile
They know what makes you cry
You offer them a ride
They leave you high and dry
You hope their dreams come true
They can't wait for you to die

Stab

My throat
My back
My heart
My butt
My rib
The air

How Could You?

Blow the whistle
Not get me a gift
Look under my skirt
Eat wet dirt
Lick the bat
Cuss the wind
Lie to your best friend
Draw the line
Spend the money
Call the cops
Halfway fart
Take the short bus
Walk all the way home
Play in the rain
Waste most the day
Show me your dick
I can't forgive you

Savor

The game
The moment
The food
The weather
The beach
The moon
The feeling
The tree
The freedom
The shower
The banter
The change
The ride
The blood
The pain
The smile
The gender
The seat
The smell
The translucent
The color
The clouds
The end

Cinderella

Ain't no princess
Ain't no supermodel
Ain't sixteen years old
Ain't that skinny
Ain't nobody's slave
Ain't losing her slipper
Ain't feeding mice
Ain't pulling the trigger
Ain't a dense blonde
Ain't covered in makeup
Ain't driving down the street
Ain't breaking the law
Ain't screaming at the top of her lungs
Ain't sitting next to you
Ain't settling for you

You Are

So sweet
So precious
So peculiar
So one of a kind
So divine
So delicious
Soul food

Great Eyes

What can hide the coming of tides?
Your mom's substantial loss?
No, your mom's bingo loss
in which her favorite sand which got tossed,
leaving grandma's homemade cornbread at a total loss
How dare she not each ranch?
I will email guitar Lance

Assholes

They only eat rare steak
They shave their pubic hair
They need to call home
They failed to fully launch
Now, grandma wants to shut her door
Some kids cause so many undue problems
Ted can't see past his momma
Drive home his brain
He can't see through the fog

You Said It

Why are you freaking out?
I told you to shut up
You left me on the liquored stairs
I'll die in my sleep before you pray
Don't' take the Lord's name in vain
Forgive all Husseins
Let's love beyond an American name
No one grew to die a God-forsaken shame

How's Your Dad?

I heard he slept with Molly Sue
She knew all the scriptures
Fuck her domain of solid gold
No one cares who she blew

Fish Not in The Sea

How many fish are in the sea?
I only see like three
They all kinda look the same
There's so much water
It's highly probable most fish drowned
Could it be they're all just asleep?
Take me to the edge of the water
Personally, I want to see all three
A closer look reveals you can't tell them apart
If only one of them would water fart
Those bubbles could tell me what
makes them truly unique
There's got to be a differentiating mark
Toss me the covert fish bait
I'll throw in four and see who takes more
Look, they're all going for it
Shit, now there's zero good fish in the sea

So Blind

Can you see me
finding my grind?
I found it post weeping,
but you're always sleeping

Can you see me
finding my grind?
I found it apart leaping,
yet you're more concerned with sweeping

Can you see me
working my grind?
I started once I got out of a bind-
"So, what," you look at me and say

Can you see me
working my grind?
I got settled in a groove once through with you,
now you're stuck just loving you

Can you see me
reaping all because of my grind?
The door opened once I shut you out,
now you can only sabotage you

BizzareR Blunts is dedicated to souls with unleashed goals. May this book of language art help you to release and share your own creative beast within. Please be encouraged to laugh at the bizarreR nature of all human beings rather than cry at the evil nature that seeks to take over humanity.

Love,
Jamie Nichole

www.ingramcontent.com/pod-product-compliance
Lightning Source LLC
Chambersburg PA
CBHW060335260626
47160CB00007B/2804